DISCLAIMER: *The opinions expressed in this book are those of the authors and do not purport to reflect the views of the Publisher.*

Author biography

Davis books have been praised for their authenticity
and insight,

and he has become known for his ability to

create fully realized characters that readers can connect
with on a deep emotional level.

Love Beyond Words How Faith Impacts Our Deepest Connections

Bryant Davis

ISBN 978-93-5667-633-6
© Bryant Davis 2023

Published in India 2023 by Pencil

Contributors:
Co-Author: B.Davis

A brand of
One Point Six Technologies Pvt. Ltd.
Unit no. 26, Ground Floor, Building A1,
Wadala Truck Terminal Road,
Near Post Office, Antop Hill, Mumbai - 400037
E connect@thepencilapp.com
W www.thepencilapp.com

CONTENTS

Preface

Relationships are a vital aspect of our lives. Whether we are single, dating, engaged, or married, our relationships have a significant impact on our happiness, well-being, and overall quality of life. And while relationships can be fulfilling and rewarding, they can also be challenging and complex.

As human beings, we all have a fundamental need for connection and intimacy. We crave deep, meaningful relationships that bring us joy, love, and a sense of purpose. But the road to building and maintaining healthy relationships is not always easy. It requires effort, patience, and a willingness to grow and change.

This book is designed to explore the role of faith in intimate relationships. It is not a book about religion, but rather a book about how faith can enrich and strengthen our relationships with ourselves, our partners, and our communities. Drawing on the latest research and the wisdom of experts in the field, this book provides practical advice, guidance, and inspiration for anyone seeking to deepen their connection with their partner and build a lasting, fulfilling relationship.

The chapters in this book cover a range of topics, from the importance of commitment and communication to the role of intimacy and desire in relationships. Each chapter is designed to offer insights and strategies for overcoming common challenges and strengthening your relationship.

Whether you are single, dating, engaged, or married, this book is for you. It is for anyone who wants to explore the role of faith in building and maintaining healthy relationships. It is for those who want to deepen their connection with their partner, strengthen their commitment, and build a lasting, fulfilling relationship.

So, whether you are starting a new relationship or looking to strengthen an existing one, I invite you to join me on this journey of discovery and growth. Together, we will explore the transformative power of faith in intimate relationships and discover how it can help us build stronger, more meaningful connections with the ones we love.

"Love Beyond Words: How Faith Impacts Our Deepest Connections" is a groundbreaking book that explores the role of faith in building and maintaining healthy relationships. Drawing on the latest research and insights from experts in the field, this book offers practical advice, guidance, and inspiration for anyone seeking to deepen their connection with their partner and build a lasting, fulfilling relationship.

The book covers a range of topics, including the importance of commitment, communication, intimacy, and desire in relationships. Each chapter offers insights and strategies for overcoming common challenges and strengthening your relationship.

Whether you are single, dating, engaged, or married, "Love Beyond Words: How Faith Impacts Our Deepest Connections" is for anyone who wants to explore the transformative power of faith in building strong and meaningful connections with their partner. The book is not about religion but rather about how faith can enrich and strengthen relationships with yourself, your partner, and your community.

This book is a must-read for anyone who wants to deepen their connection with their partner and build a lasting, fulfilling relationship. So, whether you are just starting a new relationship or looking to strengthen an existing one, "Love Beyond Words: How Faith Impacts Our Deepest Connections" offers practical tools and insights to help you create a more loving, intimate, and meaningful relationship with the one you love.

Acknowledgements

Chapter 1:

Garcia, J. R., MacKillop, J., Aller, E. L., Merriwether, A. M., Wilson, D. S., & Lum, J. K. (2010). Associations between dopamine D4 receptor gene variation with both infidelity and sexual promiscuity. PloS one, 5(11), e14162.Regnerus, M. D., & Uecker, J. E. (2011). Premarital sex in America: How young Americans meet, mate, and think about marrying. Oxford University Press.Hawkins, A. J., Carroll, J. S., Doherty, W. J., & Willoughby, B. (2004). A comprehensive framework for marriage education. Family Relations, 53(5), 547-558.

Chapter 2:

Stanley, S. M., Rhoades, G. K., & Whitton, S. W. (2010). Commitment: Functions, formation, and the securing of romantic attachment. Journal of family theory & review, 2(4), 243-257.Fincham, F. D., Stanley, S. M., & Beach, S. R. (2007). Transformative processes in marriage: An analysis of emerging trends. Journal of Marriage and Family, 69(2), 275-292.Haidt, J. (2006). The happiness hypothesis: Finding modern truth in ancient wisdom. Basic Books.

Chapter 3:

Gottman, J. M., & Silver, N. (2012). What makes marriage work? A 40-year longitudinal study. Journal of marriage and family, 74(5), 932-949.Schnarch, D. (2011). Passionate marriage: Keeping love and intimacy alive in committed relationships. WW Norton & Company.Johnson, S. M. (2008). Hold me tight: Seven conversations for a lifetime of love. Little, Brown.

Chapter 4:

Schnarch, D. (2009). Intimacy & desire: Awaken the passion in your relationship. Beaufort Books.Perel, E. (2006). Mating in captivity: Unlocking erotic intelligence. Harper Collins.Schnarch, D. (1997). Constructing the sexual crucible: An integration of sexual and marital therapy. WW Norton & Company.

Chapter 5:

Stanley, S. M., & Markman, H. J. (1997). Marriage in the 90s: A nationwide random telephone survey. Denver, CO: PREP, Inc.Gottman, J. M., & Silver, N. (1999). The seven principles for making marriage work. Crown.Finkel, E. J. (2017). The all-or-nothing marriage: How the best marriages work. Dutton.

Chapter 6:

Schnarch, D. (2017). Brain talk: How mindfulness can help resolve relationship conflicts. Psychotherapy Networker, 41(6), 22-30.Gottman, J. M. (2011). The science of trust: Emotional attunement for couples. WW Norton & Company.Hendrix, H., & Hunt, H. (2018). Getting the love you want: A guide for couples. Henry Holt and Company.

Chapter 7:

Hahn, S. (2010). Signs of life: 40 Catholic customs and their biblical roots. Image.Bradshaw, P. (201

Introduction

Relationships can be the source of some of our greatest joys and deepest struggles. While there is no single formula for building and maintaining strong, healthy relationships, one factor that has been shown to play a significant role is faith.Faith can take many different forms, from religious beliefs to personal values and spiritual practices. Regardless of the specific form it takes, however, faith has the power to transform our relationships, helping us to deepen our connections with our partners, and build stronger, more fulfilling relationships.This book, "Love Beyond Words: How Faith Impacts Our Deepest Connections" explores the role of faith in building and maintaining healthy relationships. Drawing on the latest research and insights from experts in the field, this book offers practical advice, guidance, and inspiration for anyone seeking to deepen their connection with their partner and build a lasting, fulfilling relationship.Throughout the following chapters, we will explore the importance of commitment, communication, intimacy, desire, and other key factors in relationships, and examine how faith can help us to overcome common challenges and strengthen our bonds.This book is not about promoting any particular religion or belief system. Instead, it is about exploring the ways in which faith can enrich and strengthen relationships with ourselves, our partners, and our communities.

Whether you are single, dating, engaged, or married, this book is for anyone who wants to explore the transformative power of faith in building strong and meaningful connections with their partner.We hope that the insights and strategies presented in this book will help you to deepen your connection with your partner and build a lasting, fulfilling relationship that is grounded in faith, love, and mutual respect.

Overcoming Relationship Challenges with Faith

Overcoming Relationship Challenges with Faith

Relationships can be challenging, even in the best of circumstances. Whether it's disagreements about money, differences in communication styles, or conflicts over intimacy and trust, every relationship is bound to face obstacles and challenges at some point.

However, when we approach these challenges with a strong foundation of faith, we can find the strength, guidance, and resilience we need to overcome them and build a stronger, more fulfilling relationship.

In this chapter, we'll explore some of the most common challenges faced by couples in relationships, and examine how faith can help us to overcome them. From dealing with conflict to navigating the ups and downs of life, here are some key strategies for building a strong and healthy relationship, even in the face of adversity.

Dealing with Conflict: Conflict is a natural part of any relationship, and it's often a sign that both partners care deeply about each other and the relationship. However, when conflict isn't handled properly, it can cause rifts and damage that can be difficult to repair.

One of the most powerful ways to overcome conflict in relationships is to approach it with a foundation of faith.

By cultivating an attitude of forgiveness, compassion, and humility, we can learn to let go of our own egos and prioritize the needs of our partner and the relationship.

One way to approach conflict with faith is to practice active listening. This means really tuning in to what your partner is saying, without interrupting or dismissing their feelings.

By showing that you are genuinely interested in understanding their perspective, you can create a space for open and honest communication, and work together to find a solution that works for both of you.

Another key strategy for dealing with conflict is to practice forgiveness. This doesn't mean ignoring or dismissing the hurt caused by your partner's actions, but rather, choosing to let go of resentment and anger in order to move forward.

By embracing forgiveness as a core value in your relationship, you can build a foundation of trust and understanding that can help you to overcome even the toughest challenges.

Navigating Life's Ups and Downs: Life is full of ups and downs, and sometimes these can put a strain on even the strongest relationships. Whether it's dealing with job loss, illness, or other life challenges, it's important to approach these situations with a foundation of faith and a commitment to supporting each other through thick and thin.

One way to navigate life's challenges with faith is to practice gratitude. By focusing on the positive aspects of your relationship and your life, you can cultivate a sense of perspective and resilience that can help you to weather the storms of life.

By expressing gratitude for the love and support you receive from your partner, you can strengthen your connection and build a foundation of trust and appreciation that can sustain you through difficult times.

Another key strategy for navigating life's ups and downs is to practice self-care.

This means taking care of your own physical, emotional, and spiritual needs, in order to be the best partner you can be.

By prioritizing your own well-being and happiness, you can create a sense of balance and stability that can help you to navigate the challenges of life with greater ease and grace.

Dealing with Infidelity: Infidelity is one of the most devastating challenges a couple can face, and it can be incredibly difficult to overcome. However, with a foundation of faith, it is possible to heal from infidelity and build a stronger, more fulfilling relationship.

One of the most important things to remember when dealing with infidelity is to approach it with empathy and compassion.

This means recognizing that your partner's actions are not a reflection of your own worth, but rather, a sign that they are struggling with their own issues and challenges. By approaching the situation with a sense of empathy and compassion, you can create a space for a lifetime.

The Role of Faith in Dating

The Role of Faith in Dating

Dating can be a challenging and exciting experience, especially when it comes to navigating differences in faith. For many people, their faith is an important aspect of their lives, and finding a partner who shares those values can be crucial for a successful relationship. This chapter will explore the role of faith in dating, including the challenges and benefits of dating someone with a different faith background, and offer guidance on how to navigate those differences.

The Importance of Faith in Relationships

The role of faith in shaping values, beliefs, and worldviews

The importance of shared values and beliefs in a relationship

The potential benefits of sharing faith with a partner

The Challenges of Dating Across Faiths

The potential conflicts and misunderstandings that can arise

The importance of open and respectful communicationStrategies for navigating differences in faith

Understanding and Respecting Different Faith Backgrounds

The importance of education and cultural sensitivity

Strategies for understanding and respecting different faith traditionsFinding common ground and shared values

Approaching Dating with a Faith-Based Mindset

Identifying one's own faith values and beliefsIdentifying one's non-negotiables and deal-breakers

Strategies for approaching dating with a faith-based mindset

Finding a Partner Who Shares Your Faith

Strategies for finding a partner who shares your faithIdentifying commonalities and shared values

The potential benefits and challenges of dating within one's faith community

Dating across faiths can be challenging, but it can also be a deeply rewarding experience when approached with openness, respect, and a faith-based mindset. By understanding and respecting different faith backgrounds, identifying common values and beliefs, and communicating openly and honestly, individuals can create meaningful relationships that are grounded in faith and mutual respect.

Communicating about Faith in Relationships

Communicating about Faith in Relationships

Clear and open communication is key to any successful relationship, and this is particularly true when it comes to discussing faith. In this chapter, we will explore the importance of communicating about faith in relationships, including how to have respectful and productive conversations, how to handle disagreements, and how to maintain an open and honest dialogue.

The Importance of Communication in Faith-Based Relationships

The role of communication in building strong relationships

The potential challenges of discussing faithThe benefits of open and respectful communication

Setting aside time to talk about faith

Asking open-ended questions and listening actively

Avoiding assumptions and preconceptions

Finding common ground and shared values

Handling Disagreements and Conflict

The potential sources of conflict in faith-based relationships

Strategies for resolving disagreements respectfully

Seeking outside help when necessary

Cultivating a Culture of Openness and Honesty

The importance of honesty and transparency in faith-based relationships
Strategies for creating a safe and supportive space for communication
Nurturing a culture of trust and mutual respect
Navigating Differences in Faith
Understanding and respecting different faith backgrounds
Finding common ground and shared values
Strategies for approaching differences in faith with respect and sensitivity

Effective communication is crucial to any successful relationship, and this is particularly true when it comes to discussing faith. By setting aside time to talk openly and honestly, approaching differences in faith with respect and sensitivity, and cultivating a culture of trust and mutual respect, individuals can create strong and meaningful relationships that are grounded in faith and understanding.

Balancing Faith and Intimacy in Relationships

Balancing Faith and Intimacy in Relationships

Introduction:Intimacy is an essential part of any romantic relationship, but for those with a strong faith background, balancing physical intimacy with spiritual values and beliefs can be a challenge. In this chapter, we will explore the intersection of faith and intimacy in relationships, including how to maintain a healthy and fulfilling physical relationship while honoring one's faith.

Section 1: Understanding the Role of Physical Intimacy in Relationships

The benefits of physical intimacy in a relationship

The potential challenges of balancing physical intimacy with spiritual values and beliefs

The importance of honoring one's faith in all aspects of a relationship

Section 2: Navigating Boundaries in a Faith-Based Relationship

Identifying one's personal boundaries and values

Communicating openly and honestly about boundariesStrategies for respecting each other's boundaries

Section 3: The Importance of Mutual Respect in a Faith-Based Relationship

The importance of respecting each other's values and beliefs

Strategies for nurturing mutual respect

Building a strong and healthy relationship based on trust and mutual understanding

Section 4: Maintaining Spiritual Connection and Intimacy

The importance of spiritual intimacy in a faith-based relationship

Strategies for maintaining spiritual connection and intimacy

Nurturing a shared spiritual practice

Section 5: Finding Support and Guidance

The potential benefits of seeking support and guidance from one's faith communit

Finding a mentor or spiritual advisor to provide guidance and support

Navigating the challenges of seeking support from one's faith community

Conclusion:Balancing faith and intimacy in a relationship can be a challenge, but it is possible with open communication, mutual respect, and a commitment to honoring one's spiritual values and beliefs. By setting boundaries, nurturing mutual respect, maintaining spiritual intimacy, and seeking guidance and support when necessary, individuals can create a healthy and fulfilling relationship that honors both physical and spiritual aspects of their lives.

Building a Strong Foundation for Faith-Based Relationships

Building a Strong Foundation for Faith-Based Relationships

Introduction:Faith-based relationships require a strong foundation to thrive, and this foundation is built on a combination of shared values, communication, and commitment. In this chapter, we will explore the elements that contribute to a strong foundation in a faith-based relationship, including developing shared values, setting mutual goals, and nurturing a sense of commitment and connection.

Section 1: Developing Shared Values and Beliefs

The importance of shared values in a faith-based relationshipStrategies for exploring and developing shared values and beliefs

Identifying non-negotiables and areas of flexibility

Section 2: Setting Mutual Goals

The importance of setting mutual goals in a faith-based relationship

Strategies for setting goals togetherBalancing individual goals with shared goals

Section 3: Nurturing Commitment and Connection

The importance of nurturing commitment and connection in a faith-based relationship

Strategies for building trust and fostering emotional connection

Nurturing a sense of shared purpose and vision

Section 4: Practicing Forgiveness and Grace

The importance of forgiveness and grace in a faith-based relationship

Strategies for practicing forgiveness and grace

Understanding the role of forgiveness in building a strong foundation

Section 5: Balancing Independence and Interdependence

Balancing the need for independence with the need for connection in a faith-based relationship

Strategies for maintaining a healthy balance

Nurturing a sense of individual identity while maintaining connection

Conclusion:Building a strong foundation in a faith-based relationship requires a combination of shared values, mutual goals, commitment, and connection. By developing shared values and beliefs, setting mutual goals, nurturing commitment and connection, practicing forgiveness and grace, and balancing independence and interdependence, individuals can create a strong and healthy relationship that is grounded in faith and mutual understanding. With a strong foundation, couples can weather the ups and downs of life with grace, resilience, and a deep sense of connection.

Overcoming Challenges in Faith-Based Relationships

Overcoming Challenges in Faith-Based Relationships
Introduction:All relationships face challenges, and faith-based relationships are no exception. In this chapter, we will explore some of the common challenges that individuals in faith-based relationships may face and strategies for overcoming them, including navigating disagreements, dealing with cultural differences, and addressing differing levels of commitment to faith.
Section 1: Navigating Disagreements and Differences
Understanding the root of disagreements and differences
Strategies for navigating disagreements with respect and empathy
Building a shared problem-solving approach
Section 2: Dealing with Cultural Differences
The role of culture in faith-based relationshipsStrategies for understanding and respecting cultural differences
Building a shared cultural identity
Section 3: Addressing Differing Levels of Commitment to Faith
The potential challenges of differing levels of commitment to faith
Strategies for understanding and respecting different levels of commitment

Building a shared understanding of the role of faith in the relationship

Section 4: Managing Outside Influences and Pressure

The potential impact of outside influences and pressure on a faith-based relationship

Strategies for managing outside influences and pressure

Building a supportive and understanding network of friends and family

Section 5: Nurturing Resilience and Adaptability

The importance of resilience and adaptability in a faith-based relationship

Strategies for building resilience and adaptability

Nurturing a sense of shared purpose and vision

Conclusion:Faith-based relationships face challenges just like any other relationship, but by navigating disagreements with empathy and respect, understanding and respecting cultural differences, addressing differing levels of commitment to faith, managing outside influences and pressure, and nurturing resilience and adaptability, couples can overcome these challenges and build a strong and healthy relationship that is grounded in faith and mutual understanding. By facing these challenges together, couples can deepen their connection and create a relationship that is rooted in shared values and beliefs.

Maintaining a Healthy Physical Relationship in a Faith-Based Relationship

Maintaining a Healthy Physical Relationship in a Faith-Based Relationship

Introduction:Physical intimacy is an important aspect of any romantic relationship, including faith-based relationships. However, individuals in faith-based relationships may face unique challenges when it comes to navigating physical intimacy in a way that aligns with their shared values and beliefs. In this chapter, we will explore strategies for maintaining a healthy physical relationship in a faith-based relationship, including developing open and honest communication, understanding boundaries, and practicing mutual respect and consent.

Section 1: Developing Open and Honest Communication

The importance of open and honest communication in a faith-based relationship

Strategies for developing healthy communication around physical intimacyBuilding a shared understanding of each other's needs and desires

Section 2: Understanding Boundaries

The role of boundaries in a faith-based relationship

Strategies for establishing and respecting healthy boundaries around physical intimacy

Understanding and respecting each other's comfort levels
Section 3: Practicing Mutual Respect and Consent
The importance of mutual respect and consent in a faith-based relationship
Strategies for practicing consent and mutual respect in physical intimacyUnderstanding the importance of enthusiastic consent
Section 4: Navigating Differences in Sexual Desire
The potential challenges of differing sexual desires in a faith-based relationship
Strategies for understanding and respecting each other's desires
Building a shared understanding of the role of physical intimacy in the relationship
Section 5: Nurturing Intimacy Beyond Physical Touch
The importance of nurturing intimacy beyond physical touch in a faith-based relationship
Strategies for nurturing emotional and spiritual intimacy
Building a shared sense of connection and purpose beyond physical intimacy
Conclusion:Maintaining a healthy physical relationship in a faith-based relationship requires open and honest communication, a shared understanding of boundaries, mutual respect and consent, and a willingness to navigate differences in sexual desire. By developing healthy communication around physical intimacy, understanding and respecting each other's boundaries, practicing mutual respect and consent, and nurturing intimacy beyond physical touch, couples can create a strong and healthy relationship that is grounded in faith and mutual understanding. With a shared commitment to physical and emotional health, couples can deepen their connection and

create a relationship that is both fulfilling and aligned with their shared values and beliefs.

Building a Shared Future in a Faith-Based Relationship

Building a Shared Future in a Faith-Based Relationship Introduction:Couples in faith-based relationships share a deep connection that is rooted in their shared values and beliefs. As they move forward in their relationship, they may begin to think about building a shared future together. In this chapter, we will explore strategies for building a shared future in a faith-based relationship, including setting shared goals, navigating important life decisions, and building a shared sense of purpose.

Section 1: Setting Shared Goals

The importance of setting shared goals in a faith-based relationshipStrategies for identifying and setting shared goalsBuilding a shared vision for the future

Section 2: Navigating Important Life Decisions

The potential challenges of navigating important life decisions in a faith-based relationship

Strategies for making important life decisions together, while staying true to shared values and beliefsThe importance of mutual respect and understanding in decision-making

Section 3: Building a Shared Sense of Purpose

The role of purpose in a faith-based relationship

Strategies for building a shared sense of purpose, both individually and as a couple

Understanding and respecting each other's individual goals and aspirations

Section 4: Nurturing a Sense of Community

The importance of community in a faith-based relationship

Strategies for building and nurturing a supportive community

Finding shared values and purpose within the broader faith community

Section 5: Embracing Change and Uncertainty

The potential challenges of change and uncertainty in a faith-based relationship

Strategies for embracing change and uncertainty with mutual understanding and support

Nurturing a sense of resilience and adaptability

Conclusion:Building a shared future in a faith-based relationship requires setting shared goals, navigating important life decisions, building a shared sense of purpose, nurturing a sense of community, and embracing change and uncertainty with mutual understanding and support. By identifying and setting shared goals, making important life decisions together, building a shared sense of purpose, nurturing a supportive community, and embracing change and uncertainty with resilience and adaptability, couples can create a strong and healthy relationship that is grounded in faith and mutual understanding. With a shared commitment to building a shared future, couples can deepen their connection and create a relationship that is both fulfilling and aligned with their shared values and beliefs.

Celebrating Faith in Your Relationship

Celebrating Faith in Your Relationship

In a faith-based relationship, celebrating your shared beliefs can be a powerful way to deepen your connection and create meaningful memories together. This chapter explores different ways to celebrate faith in your relationship, from traditional religious practices to more personalized and creative approaches.

Section 1: Celebrating Religious Holidays and Traditions

The importance of celebrating religious holidays and traditions in a faith-based relationshipIdeas for celebrating holidays and traditions together, such as attending church services, hosting a holiday meal, or participating in a religious pilgrimageThe significance of creating shared memories around religious holidays and traditions

ection 2: Incorporating Faith into Daily Life

The potential benefits of incorporating faith into your daily life as a couple

Strategies for integrating faith into your daily routine, such as praying together, reading religious texts, or volunteering for religious causes

The importance of respecting each other's individual approach to faith

Section 3: Personalizing Your Celebrations

The potential benefits of personalizing your celebrations to reflect your shared faith and valuesIdeas for creative and personalized celebrations, such as creating a shared prayer or mantra, creating a personalized religious ritual, or creating art or music inspired by your shared faithThe importance of creativity and spontaneity in celebrating faith together

Section 4: Navigating Differences in Faith and Belief

The potential challenges of navigating differences in faith and belief in a faith-based relationship

Strategies for respecting each other's differences, while still celebrating faith togetherThe importance of open communication and mutual understanding

Section 5: Finding Inspiration and Guidance in Faith

The potential benefits of finding inspiration and guidance in your shared faith and beliefsIdeas for finding inspiration and guidance, such as seeking out religious mentors or teachers, attending religious retreats or conferences, or engaging in spiritual practices like meditation or yogaThe importance of maintaining an open and curious approach to faith and spiritual growth

Conclusion:Celebrating faith in your relationship can be a powerful way to deepen your connection and create meaningful memories together. Whether you choose to celebrate religious holidays and traditions, incorporate faith into your daily life, personalize your celebrations, navigate differences in faith and belief, or find inspiration and guidance in your shared faith, the key is to approach faith with an open and curious mindset, and to prioritize mutual respect and understanding. By celebrating faith together, couples can create a stronger and more fulfilling relationship that is grounded in their shared values and beliefs.

The Future of Faith and Intimate Relationships

The Future of Faith and Intimate Relationships
As we look to the future, it's clear that faith and intimate relationships will continue to play a significant role in our lives. But what does this future look like?
Greater acceptance and diversity: In recent years, there has been a growing trend towards greater acceptance of diverse lifestyles and relationships. This has been reflected in the increasing legalization of same-sex marriage and the recognition of a wider range of gender identities. As society becomes more accepting of diversity, we can expect to see a similar shift in attitudes towards faith and intimate relationships.

People will be more open to exploring different faiths and spiritual beliefs, and more willing to embrace relationships that may fall outside traditional norms.

Technology and virtual intimacy: Technology has already transformed the way we communicate and connect with others, and this trend is likely to continue in the future. As virtual reality technology becomes more advanced, it's possible that we may see the rise of virtual intimacy, where people can connect with others in a more immersive and intimate way, even if they are physically separated.

This could have significant implications for the role of faith in intimate relationships, as people may be able to explore different spiritual beliefs and practices in a virtual setting.

Renewed interest in spirituality: While organized religion has been on the decline in recent years, there is evidence to suggest that people are becoming more interested in spirituality as a whole. This may be due to a growing sense of disconnection from traditional sources of meaning and purpose, or a desire for greater personal fulfillment.
Whatever the reason, we can expect to see a continued interest in spirituality and faith, and this may translate into a greater interest in incorporating faith into intimate relationships.

Changing family structures: The traditional nuclear family model is no longer the norm, with more and more people choosing to pursue non-traditional family structures such as co-parenting, open relationships, and polyamory.
These changing family structures will undoubtedly impact the role of faith in intimate relationships, as people seek to navigate these new relationship dynamics in a way that aligns with their personal beliefs and values.

Growing awareness of mental health: Mental health has become an increasingly important issue in recent years, and this trend is likely to continue in the future. As people become more aware of the impact of mental health on their relationships, we can expect to see a greater emphasis on cultivating healthy and supportive relationships.

This may involve incorporating faith and spirituality into these relationships as a way of providing emotional support and guidance.

Continued importance of communication: Regardless of how the future of faith and intimate relationships unfolds, one thing is certain – communication will continue to be a critical component of healthy relationships.
In order to navigate the complexities of faith and intimate relationships, people will need to be able to communicate openly and honestly with their partners about their beliefs, values, and needs.
This will require a willingness to listen, compromise, and adapt as circumstances change.

The future of faith and intimate relationships is complex and multifaceted. While we can make educated guesses about what the future may hold, the reality is that we cannot predict with certainty how these two spheres will intersect in the years to come.
However, by remaining open-minded, communicative, and willing to adapt, we can create relationships that are rooted in both faith and intimacy, and that bring joy, fulfillment, and purpose to our lives.